The Pandas Next Door

By Vickie An
Illustrated by Guy Wolek

Publishing Credits
Rachelle Cracchiolo, M.S.Ed., *Publisher*
Emily R. Smith, M.A.Ed., *VP of Content Development*
Véronique Bos, *Creative Director*
Dani Neiley, *Associate Editor*
Kevin Pham, *Graphic Designer*

Image Credits
Illustrated by Guy Wolek

Library of Congress Cataloging-in-Publication Data
Names: An, Vickie, author. | Wolek, Guy, illustrator.
Title: The pandas next door / by Vickie An ; illustrated by Guy Wolek.
Description: Huntington Beach, CA : Teacher Created Materials, [2022] | Audience: Grades 2-3. | Summary: "The Panda family's new neighbors are not very welcoming. But if anyone can change their minds, it's Riley!"-- Provided by publisher.
Identifiers: LCCN 2021051037 (print) | LCCN 2021051038 (ebook) | ISBN 9781087601823 (paperback) | ISBN 9781087631868 (ebook)
Subjects: LCSH: Readers (Primary) | LCGFT: Readers (Publications)
Classification: LCC PE1119.2 .A527 2022 (print) | LCC PE1119.2 (ebook) | DDC 428.6/2--dc23/eng/20211029
LC record available at https://lccn.loc.gov/2021051037
LC ebook record available at https://lccn.loc.gov/2021051038

5482 Argosy Avenue
Huntington Beach, CA 92649
www.tcmpub.com

ISBN 978-1-0876-0182-3
© 2022 Teacher Created Materials, Inc.
This book may not be reproduced or distributed in any way without prior written consent from the publisher.
Printed in Malaysia. THU001.46774

Table of Contents

Chapter One:
  Pride Place 4

Chapter Two:
  Birds of a Feather 10

Chapter Three:
  The Case of the Missing Pearls 16

Chapter Four:
  Riley, the Hero 22

About Us 28

Chapter One

≪ ≪ ≪ ≫ ≫ ≫

Pride Place

"Look, guys!" cried Riley. "We're here!" The second grader peered out the truck window and grinned. It was moving day. The Panda family had just pulled up to their new house.

Riley's mom got a new teaching job in Pride Place. The new town was far from Bamboo Bluff, where Riley was born. She felt sad at first. Leaving the city and her friends was hard. It was the only home she had ever known. But her mom told her that Pride Place would feel like home soon.

Everyone jumped out of the truck. Riley's big brother, Mason, stretched his arms high above his head and yawned. He grabbed his basketball out of the back. Riley and her mom started unloading the boxes. Riley put on her favorite purple detective cap. She loved mysteries and wanted to be a detective when she grew up. She eyed her new street. It seemed quiet for a Sunday afternoon. Too quiet.

Suddenly, Riley spotted someone at the house next door. A girl poked her head outside. She looked like she might be Riley's age. A new friend, maybe? Riley's mom said their new neighbors are peacocks. Riley had never met a peacock before. She raised her hand to wave. Then, the girl's parents came to the door.

"Come inside, Poppy. Leave these city pandas alone," said her father. He frowned in Riley's direction. Poppy vanished behind the door.

"Why didn't they say *hi*?" Riley wondered aloud. But before she could think about it too much, she heard her mom calling her. "Coming, Mama!" she answered. *It's OK,* she thought. *Tomorrow is a new day.*

Chapter Two

‹ ‹ ‹ › › ›

Birds of a Feather

Riley peeked inside the classroom. Today was the first day of second grade at her new school. She felt excited and nervous. A million questions ran through her head. Would she like it? Would the other students like her? Would she fit in?

"Have a great first day, honey!" Mama Panda said. She and Mrs. Lopez, Riley's teacher, had just finished talking in the hallway. "What do I always say?"

"You say to always be kind," Riley replied. Mama Panda nodded. She gave Riley a big bear hug. Then, Mrs. Lopez led Riley inside.

"Class, this is Riley. Her family just moved here from Bamboo Bluff. Please make her feel welcome," Mrs. Lopez said. She pointed to an empty desk. "Riley, you can sit next to Poppy."

Riley remembered Poppy from yesterday. Riley plopped down. "Hi!" she said. "You live next door, right?"

Poppy opened her mouth to answer. But one of her friends stopped her.

"Poppy, she's not from around here," whispered the other girl. Poppy looked embarrassed and turned away quickly.

"Don't mind them, Riley," called a voice from behind. Riley spun around in her chair. She saw a friendly face smiling at her. "I'm Chloe, and this is Claire," the girl said. The student next to her waved. "Want to be friends?"

From then on, Riley, Chloe, and Claire did everything together. It just so happened they all loved mysteries. Riley thought that maybe she was going to like it here.

Chapter Three

‹ ‹ ‹ › › ›

The Case of the Missing Pearls

"Wow, what a cool detective kit!" Claire said. Riley beamed with pride. Grandma and Grandpa Panda gave it to her for her birthday last year. The kit was Riley's most prized possession. She couldn't wait for her turn for show and tell.

Riley looked around to see what everyone else brought to school. Her eyes landed on Poppy, who was under her desk. "Where is it? Where is it?" Poppy kept mumbling.

"What's wrong, Poppy?" Riley asked.

"It's my mom's pearl necklace," Poppy replied. "I can't find it." Her eyes filled with tears.

Riley gave Poppy a comforting pat. "Don't worry," Riley told her. "I'm on the case!" She took out the magnifying glass from her detective kit. Then, she rounded up her classmates to help.

"Let's retrace your footsteps," Riley said to Poppy. They looked all over the classroom. But the necklace wasn't there. They looked in the hallway. But the necklace wasn't there, either. They looked in the cafeteria. No necklace. Where could it be?

Then, Poppy remembered something. "I played on the swings before school today," she said.

Mrs. Lopez walked the class out to the playground. Riley sprinted to the swings and searched the grass. Soon, she spotted something white. It was the pearl necklace!

"I found it!" Riley shouted, holding up the pearls. Riley's classmates cheered. Poppy sighed with relief. Mystery solved.

Chapter Four

‹ ‹ ‹ › › ›

Riley, the Hero

Poppy held her mom's pearl necklace. She turned to Riley. "Thank you for helping me find my mom's necklace," Poppy said.

Riley grinned. "You're welcome, Poppy," she replied. "I'm always happy to help."

Riley was so kind, thought Poppy. But Poppy had not been very nice at all. Her mom and dad didn't want her making friends with Riley. Her friends didn't think it was a good idea either. Poppy decided they were all wrong.

"Riley, I wasn't very kind to you when you first moved here," Poppy said. "I'm so sorry. Can we still be friends?"

"Sure!" Riley said. She was glad Poppy wanted to be friends.

Later, Poppy's parents came to pick her up from school. Poppy told them how Riley had saved the day. Poppy's mom thought about it as she put her pearl necklace on. "Preston, maybe we should give the Pandas a chance," she said to Poppy's dad.

"You're right, Pepper," he agreed. "We have not been very welcoming. Let's fix that."

That afternoon, Poppy's family went next door. The Panda family welcomed their neighbors with open arms.

They even tried some of Grandma Panda's famous earthworm cookies. Laughter filled the room.

Riley smiled. She had finally met a peacock. Pride Place was beginning to feel like home.

About Us

The Author
Vickie An grew up in Houston, Texas. But she's lived all over the world. She enjoys traveling, trying new foods, and exploring with her daughter, Zoe. She loves pandas, too.

The Illustrator
Guy Wolek has been an artist for over 30 years. He has done a variety of jobs with his skills, such as sketch artist, illustrator, and art director. Guy enjoys creating art.